This book belongs to:

_____

_____

·GRANDPA CUTLASS·

SCHOOL FOR BANDITS
A JONATHAN CAPE BOOK 978 1 780 08000 0

Published in Great Britain by Jonathan Cape,
an imprint of Random House Children's Books
A Random House Group Company

This edition published 2011

1 3 5 7 9 10 8 6 4 2

RANDOM HOUSE CHILDREN'S BOOKS 61–63 Uxbridge Road, London W5 5SA

www.**kids**at**randomhouse**.co.uk
www.**rbooks**.co.uk

Addresses for companies within The Random House Group Limited
can be found at: www.randomhouse.co.uk/offices.htm

THE RANDOM HOUSE GROUP Limited Reg. No. 954009

A CIP catalogue record for this book is available from the British Library.

Printed in China

To Imi,
my sister in crime,
& winsome Betsy
the flapjack bandit!

·UNCLE WHISKERS·

SCHOOL
for
BANDITS

MRS RACCOON · RALPH · MR RACCOON

HANNAH SHAW

JONATHAN CAPE • LONDON

Mr and Mrs Raccoon were worried about their son Ralph.

He *looked* perfectly normal,

BUT...

...he didn't act normal at all.

He was disturbingly
well-behaved,

clean and tidy,

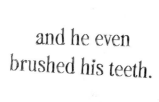

and he even
brushed his teeth.

Not only that, but he was shockingly polite.

"We didn't bring you up to be like this," sighed his dad.

"How will you ever become a great raccoon bandit like Grandpa Cutlass or Uncle Whiskers?

It's time you learned some bad manners . . .

We're sending you to Bandit School."

When Ralph arrived at Bandit School, he saw at once that he wasn't going to fit in.

All the other raccoons looked bigger, bolder and really bad!

THROW YOUR FOOD!

He didn't like lunch time either,

or the sports activities that everyone else was so enthusiastic about.

The first week at school was one disaster after another.

He failed the science test.

He failed art.

And he failed to impress Mrs Mischief.

"Ralph Raccoon! You MUST learn to take things that aren't yours WITHOUT asking," she scolded.

At the end of term, Mrs Mischief
gave Ralph his report to take home.
"Not much improvement,"
she said with a frown.

REPORT
RALPH RACCOON
very well
BEHAVED
FAR too
POLITE

Then she gave them each a big sack.

"Whoever fills their sack with the most loot during the holidays will win the BEST BANDIT IN SCHOOL competition. Good luck, everyone!"

PRIZE

Who will win the BEST BANDIT in school competition?

"B is for "BOO!"

A is for Asking is not Necessary

D is for Demolition

Ralph's loot sack stayed empty
throughout the school holidays.

Meanwhile all the other raccoons
were busy trying to fill theirs.

"Don't you want to go and play?"
asked his mum.

Ralph shook his head:
he didn't want to cause trouble.

On the first day of the new term, Ralph picked up
his empty sack with a heavy heart and started to walk to school.

It just didn't seem *right* to try and
win a competition by being really bad.

Ralph was so deep in thought that he almost
bumped into a flustered-looking poodle.

"What a lovely young raccoon," said the poodle, and gave him pawfuls of sticky sweets.

"Excuse me, can I help you?" asked Ralph politely.

"My HAIR!" she wailed. "It's a disaster!"

Ralph pointed her in the direction of the grooming parlour.

He put the sweets in his sack and walked on.

As he crossed the park,
he gave a friendly wave
to a family having a picnic.

But something wasn't right.
They were jumping
up and down, shouting:
"Fluffy!
Come down!"

Poor Fluffy was clinging helplessly to a tree.
Quickly Ralph climbed up to rescue her.

"How kind!" said the family,
and they gave Ralph
lots of yummy goodies
from their picnic hamper.

Ralph put the goodies
in his sack and walked on.

As he strolled
past the bandstand,
Ralph noticed it was empty.

He spotted the entire brass band
standing at the edge of the duck pond.

They weren't playing
their usual happy tunes.

"What's wrong?"
asked Ralph.

"Our music blew into the pond!"
wailed the conductor.

"Don't worry!"
said Ralph. "I'll get it!"

And he swam out to fetch it.

"What a hero," tooted the band,
and they loaded Ralph
with armfuls of treats.

He gratefully added the treats
to his collection and turned towards school.

By now the sack was so heavy,
Ralph could hardly lift it.
With much tugging and struggling
he dragged it into the classroom.

The other bigger, bolder,
much badder raccoons
stared in astonishment.

Not one of them had
done nearly as well.

"Well done, Ralph!" said a rather surprised-looking Mrs Mischief.

"You've won the BEST BANDIT IN SCHOOL competition!"

Ralph had his photo taken, and Mrs Mischief told his proud parents, who couldn't stop smiling.

"Just like his Grandpa Cutlass," beamed his dad.

The other raccoons were puzzled
and just a little bit jealous.

"Tell us how you did it,"
they begged . . .

Ralph grinned at his new friends.

"Well, first you have to say
'Please...'"

And that's just what they did.